CONFIDENTIAL
Appendix "E" of the official U.S. Navy Report

"EXTRAGRAVITATIONAL PROPULSION FOR MILITARY PURPOSES"

On May 23, 1954, and October 17, 1954, two piloted extragravitational projectiles developed by the United States Navy were successfully impelled beyond the earth's gravitational field and guided to the moon.

The first projectile crashed on the satellite's surface. Its pilot, Lt. Daniel More Butler, USN, is missing and presumed dead. The second projectile returned.

Appendix "E" reproduces the contents of one hundred and seven sheets of paper in Lieutenant Butler's handwriting, found by the pilot of the second projectile at the scene of the crash.

The papers purport to describe his encounter with "Inhabitants" of the moon and his descent with them into their land under the surface of the satellite.

ALSO BY HERMAN WOUK

THE
"LOMOKOME"
PAPERS

HERMAN WOUK

Illustrated by Harry Bennett

Herman Wouk

THE

"LOMOKOME"

PAPERS

Published by POCKET BOOKS *New York*

THE "LOMOKOME" PAPERS

A *Pocket Book* edition
1st printing . . . . March, 1968

This *Pocket Book* edition is printed from
brand-new plates made from newly set, clear, easy-to-read type.
Pocket Book editions are published by Pocket Books, a division of
Simon & Schuster, Inc., 630 Fifth Avenue, New York, N.Y. 10020.
Trademarks registered in the United States and other countries.

Preface to the Paperback Edition

This tale of a moon voyage, my one effort at science fiction, was written in 1949, just before the start of the sea narrative that became *The Caine Mutiny*. I intended it as a mirror satire of nuclear confrontation. At the time, the Soviet Union had not yet exploded an atomic weapon, nor were scientists certain that a hydrogen bomb (then called a "hell bomb") would work. In retrospect, the tale has proven too prophetic for comfort.

Meanwhile the moon voyage, as a literary form, approaches total eclipse. In a year or two—possibly even before the present volume sees the light—it may be killed by newspaper pictures and stories of Russians or Americans treading on actual moon rubble. Eighteen years ago, a moon voyage tale was a fantasy. That is how fast the twentieth century is bulldozing away old fields of dreams.

Storytellers have been writing about moon journeys for thousands of years. A charming book on the subject that I read by chance, Marjorie Nicolson's *Voyages to the Moon,* spurred me to try the form. The moon trip can be a romantic adventure, a social satire, or a utopian sermon. Mine is a mixture of these. *Lomokome* in Hebrew means Utopia or Nowhere. The novel starts in the dry vein of a Defoe hoax, and gradually slips into the mirror satire of Reasonable War, and the modest proposal of Death Day. It dodges the problem of propulsion, as all the moon voyages do. My pseudo-solution resembles that of H. G. Wells in *First Men in the Moon,* perhaps the best of the fictional journeys.

Essentially this tale derives from both *A Modest Proposal* and the chapter in *Erewhon* on musical banks. It was planned at first to be as long as *Erewhon,* scanning all postwar society with lunar parody and mirroring. I was much under the spell of Samuel Butler, that prince of English prose. This briefer work, centered on the atomic war theme, was the outcome. It was virtually the only time one of my literary undertakings contracted instead of expanding. I wish it would happen more often. Perhaps readers do, too.

Scanning this tale again in the decade of Gemini, Surveyor, missile crises, and Viet Nam, I am sobered by the speed with which truth is overtaking my grim fiction. But at least we are still here, still seeking a way out, and—as I write this—still with a little time left.

HERMAN WOUK

Washington
27 May 1967

THE
"LOMOKOME"
PAPERS

Appendix "E" of the official U.S. Navy Report

"EXTRAGRAVITATIONAL
PROPULSION
FOR MILITARY PURPOSES"

Released in advance of the main report by
direction of the Chief of Naval Operations.

*Preface by Professor V. W. Robinson,
of the Montana Institute of Technology.*

FOREWORD
by the Chief of Naval Operations

The requirements of military security do not
permit the release to the general public at this time of
Extragravitational Propulsion for Military Purposes,
known by the short title of the Robinson Report.

An unfortunate and misleading breach of

security by one newspaper has caused such widespread public commotion that it is deemed necessary to release at once, and separately, Appendix E of the report. The President of the United States and the Secretary of Defense have concurred in this decision.

The preface by Professor V. W. Robinson is an unofficial expression of his opinion regarding Appendix E. The Navy's official views in the matter are in substantial agreement therewith.

This in no sense detracts from the unprecedented and historic gallantry of Lieutenant Daniel More Butler, USN, who made the supreme sacrifice in Phase Able of the operation herein alluded to.

The main Report, with appendices, will be released by direction of the President at the earliest practicable time consistent with over-all national security.

Admiral Jonathan S. Wells, USN.

Navy Department, 1 December 1955.

PREFACE

The balance between the needs of military secrecy and the need (in a democracy) of a well-informed public is precarious.

In August, 1945, the United States Army released the Smyth Report on the atomic bomb, containing a detailed and accurate account of the making of that startling new implement of war, withholding only a few crucial technical details. It was believed that world scientists everywhere knew, or were capable of inferring from the very existence of the bomb, all the facts in the Smyth Report.

Since then there has been speculation, extending to official circles, as to whether the release of the Smyth Report did not give potentially hostile powers credit for more scientific knowledge than they possessed—or, to put it plainly, whether in fulfilling the duty of informing the public, the Smyth Report did not inadvertently serve as a break in secrecy.

Considerations of this nature have determined the withholding of the report, *Extragravitational Propulsion for Military Purposes,* which was completed and submitted to the President on January 3, 1955.

It is no longer advisable or practicable, however, to suppress certain facts about the Project. They must be publicized to counteract the widespread half-truths, rumors and wild inventions arising from the series of "disclosures" printed in the St. Louis Journal-Herald on November 11, 12, 13 and 14, 1955.

These articles were sensational, fanciful and, in large measure, false. Printing them without consulting or warning responsible authorities was a breach of the ethics of American journalism, as well as a blow to the nation's security.

The following erroneous impressions are now widespread and must be refuted: that the United States Navy has made many expeditions to the moon and can make more at will; that a naval lieutenant is now on the moon, alive but lost, and has been abandoned to his fate by the Navy; and, wildest of all, that a race of beings has been discovered on the moon, hardly different from humankind, but vastly ahead of us in scientific knowledge and possessed of incredibly powerful military weapons.

The following facts are correct. On May 23, 1954, and October 17, 1954, two piloted extragravitational projectiles developed by the United States Navy were successfully impelled beyond the earth's gravitational field and guided to the moon. The first projectile crashed on the satellite's surface near the crater Copernicus. Its pilot, Lieutenant Daniel More Butler, USN, the first man in history to travel beyond the earth's gravitational field, is missing and is presumed dead. The second projectile (the name of the pilot is withheld for reasons of security) returned. The pilot of the second projectile was able to reconnoiter the scene of Lieutenant Butler's crash, in a manner limited by the cumbersome equipment necessary for such a task. His report indicated the reasons for the crash, which cannot be disclosed here. It also included almost certain evidence that Lieutenant Butler is dead.

The Navy has been working on a major scale since 1943 on the problem of extragravitational propulsion for military purposes. It was not planned to disclose the actual achievement of flight outside the gravitational field of earth until the recent relaxation of international tension had gone much further. The public will readily see that the publication of the Journal-Herald articles has forced on the government a substantial change in policy.

No details of the two successful flights, nor of current work in the Rhododendron Project, nor of the correct solution to the problem of extragravitational propulsion, can be given at this time. Parenthetically, it may be stated that one of the egregious inaccuracies in the Journal-Herald articles was the statement that atomic-powered rockets were used in the moon flights. The projectiles are not rockets, and atomic energy plays no part in the U.S. Navy's successful system of extragravitational propulsion. The full Report will publish a discussion of the problem equal in scope and frankness to the Smyth Report on the atomic bomb. It will also contain the flight logs of Lieutenant Butler and the second pilot as Appendices C and D.

Appendix E, which is printed herewith, is the basis for the articles in the St. Louis Journal-Herald. The story of the civilian typist who smuggled a copy out of the Navy Building and attempted to peddle it to many newspapers has been sufficiently publicized. The unfortunate woman's recent suicide has closed the episode in a tragic and final fashion.

Appendix E reproduces the contents of one hundred and seven sheets of paper in Lieutenant Butler's handwriting, found by the pilot of the second projectile at the scene of the crash. Most of them were enclosed in Lieutenant Butler's leather-bound flight log. A few were found scattered inside the damaged projectile. One sheet was lying outside, wedged in rubble.

These papers are not "of a mysterious texture and quality unknown on earth." On the contrary, they are sheets from an ordinary note pad of the kind sold in five-and-ten-cent stores, as has been proved by chemical analysis. Their peculiar appearance is a result of their having been exposed to the nearly absolute zero temperature of the surface of the moon. It can be readily demonstrated that any common writing paper placed in an Onnes helium liquefier or similar apparatus will quickly acquire the same appearance.

This point is made emphatically because the "unearthly" paper has been cited as a clinching proof that the narrative of Lieutenant Butler is true; whereas there is not a scientist connected with the Rhododen-

dron Project who does not agree that it is a fiction, written down by Lieutenant Butler in a delirium caused by deprivation of oxygen.

The papers do not form a continuous narrative but are a series of fragments, which seem to be referring to the same event or series of events. They are undated and were apparently written in haste. The scrawl, though recognizably Lieutenant Butler's, is in marked contrast to the regularity of his writing in the flight log. The papers purport to describe his encounter with "inhabitants" of the moon and his descent with them into their land under the surface of the satellite.

It is my reasoned conclusion (and the same conclusion, with minor variations, has been arrived at independently by twenty-seven noted scientists who have read Appendix E and seen sample sheets) that these papers are the sad legacy of the last forty-eight or seventy-two hours of Lieutenant Butler's life, when his supply of oxygen was running out. Undoubtedly he rationed the oxygen to the minimum necessary to maintain life, hoping that help might come. He was aware of the state of readiness of Projectile Two, and he had managed to set off a distress signal which was acknowledged, in a manner not now to be divulged.

The intoxicating effect of too little oxygen is well known. Under the influence of this intoxication, Lieutenant Butler perhaps began to dwell on the fantasies about moon inhabitants he had read as a boy. It is easy to see how wishful thinking would abet such imaginings and, as the intoxication progressed and judgment weakened, would eventually generate the hallucination narrated in Appendix E. At the last, victim of his own delusory visions, he unquestionably wandered away from the projectile in search of the "moon people." It was only a question of time before he fell into one of the hundreds of deep jagged pits surrounding the projectile, damaged his breathing apparatus and perished.

It may be useful to list briefly the scientific reasons for excluding the possibility that the Butler narrative is true:

1. It is practically established that there is neither atmosphere nor moisture on the surface of the moon. Life of any known or conceivable sort cannot exist without these two environmental conditions.

2. The possibility of a livable hollow inside the satellite cannot be flatly excluded. But from what is now known of astronomy and geology, the chance of such a formation within the moon is of the order of one in thirty billions.

3. Even if that extremely unlikely formation did exist, such life as might evolve in a lunar cavern would necessarily be monstrously different from terrestrial forms. Weaker gravity, everlasting subsurface gloom and temperature fluctuations that could wipe out all earthly life in a day—to mention only the most obvious factors—would force a course of natural selec-

tion totally unlike that which has developed on earth. The idea of humanlike beings native to the moon must be dismissed. Further scientific difficulties could be listed to perhaps the number of a hundred, in regard to certain sections and paragraphs of the narrative.

The official conclusion was a painful one to reach. A lengthy tribute to Lieutenant Butler would not be in place here, but obviously this young man who secured himself a place in world history deserved every possible effort to rescue him. The departure of Projectile Two was put forward seventeen days for this purpose, at augmented risk to the pilot and despite the likelihood of highly expensive loss to the Project in the event of failure. At that time the Navy had hardly the slenderest hope of Butler's survival, but the gamble was taken. The results of the second pilot's reconnoitering ended the matter, in the view of the Navy and the civilian scientists.

The fragments that constitute Appendix E have been assembled and edited by a reserve officer, Lieutenant William T. Dawes, a writer by profession, who accepted the task at the invitation of Rear Admiral Fall, head of Naval Public Relations. Lieutenant Dawes has inserted connective passages between some of the scraps of narrative, for the purpose of clarity. These are printed in italics so as to be set off unmistakably from Lieutenant Butler's own words.

Otherwise, Appendix E contains nothing but Lieutenant Butler's papers—uncensored, unabridged and transcribed with the greatest care.

It is hoped that the publication of Appendix E will end the unfortunate situation created by the Journal-Herald articles, and will at least partly allay justified public curiosity about the Navy's extragravitational propulsion program, until such time as the full Report can be safely released.

A final word of caution seems necessary, because of the extraordinary verisimilitude of some passages in the "Lomokome" papers. The public must bear in mind that few normal people can be as persuasive as a man in the grip of a systematic delusion. The disarming artlessness and helter-skelter frankness of Lieutenant Butler's narrative are more effective than the art of the fiction writer in attaining realism. The reader must constantly remind himself of the scientific objections I have indicated above, in order to maintain perspective on these papers.

Professor V. W. Robinson

THE "LOMOKOME" PAPERS

The pilot who recovered the "Lomokome" papers took the sensible precaution of numbering consecutively in light pencil the main batch of sheets discovered in the Butler flight log, and then adding the scattered sheets to the bundle. However, on examination, it was obvious that the papers thus numbered made no sense whatever in their original order.

Rearranging them into a single consecutive narrative has proved impossible. No matter how the sheets are shuffled and reshuffled, they cannot be made to connect one to another from beginning to end. An exhaustive comparison of "last words" and "first words" of all the sheets, conducted by a staff of Navy yeomen, has established that point.

The present arrangement is made after much study and comparison with the patterns worked out by others. It differs in a few material points from the sequence worked out by the Navy before the editing task was assigned to the writer. He accepts responsibility for any inaccuracies or misleading impressions that result from the sequence here presented.

William T. Dawes, Lt., USNR

1

[Arrival in "Lomokome"—
First Impressions: Four Fragments]

...forgotten a lot already.

Actually, I should have kept notes all along, day by day and even hour by hour. But too much was happening too fast. Furthermore, I never knew for a long while but that my next hour was going to be my last, and keeping a record seemed a less urgent problem than staying alive. After it was obvious they weren't going to do me in, I suppose I became a little too interested in what was happening. I don't know how long this present spell of forced inactivity (technically I'm not imprisoned) will last. But I may as well employ it in the ancient and honorable Navy custom of writing up the log long after the fact.

I don't know whether anyone will ever see this account. I'm not going to bother with official phraseology, though I suppose everything that's happened comes under the heading of my orders: "Reconnoiter as practicable." If I ever get back I can boil it down for official purposes.

First of all, to describe my surroundings. I'm a guest, I suppose you'd call it, in the home of an eminent scientist named Vove, who bears the honorary

title of "Kaham." He has one daughter living with him, named Vovone, of whom more later. At the moment, I'm seated in one of the severe, cold, airy rooms that are ...

[*Editor's note: There is a complete break here. The narrative resumes with a fragmentary account of Lieutenant Butler's purported arrival in inhabited lunar caverns.*]

... on foot the rest of the way. But there wasn't far to go.

The "streets" are tunnels, of course, paved and brightly lighted. Some of them seem natural cave passages, for there are grotesque stalactites overhead. Others have been cut smoothly out of the rock. Regularly spaced overhead there are rings of glowing bare metal, emitting a coldish orange illumination like sodium light. The air is very dry, and frigid enough to cause your breath to smoke. I'd guess the temperature is well below freezing, but I didn't see any frozen puddles or ponds so I can't be sure. The caverns are bone-dry.

My teeth were chattering after we'd been walking five minutes. They noticed it at last, and a guard threw one of those orange cloaks over my shoulders. The effect was amazing. I was comfortable in a minute. If ever I get back home I'll have to bring along a sample of that stuff. It would be excellent for Arctic warfare. It's made wholly of inorganic minerals, they tell me. It's no heavier than linen.

As we progressed toward the center of the city, more people began to be in evidence. They were all dressed in these orange cloaks, which cover you from head to foot like a monk's robe. The people were all hurrying in the same direction as we were, streaming out of the houses hollowed into the rock on either side of the tunnel. The houses had façades carved with queer zigzag geometrical patterns. There were no vehicles in the tunnels. Everyone went on foot. They paid no attention to our party. The fact that I was a head shorter than the general population attracted hardly a glance. After walking for perhaps ten minutes we emerged into the gigantic space that they call the Central Cavern.

It's an irregularly shaped gloomy vault, about a mile and a half across at its widest. The roof is so high it is lost in gloom, except for some tremendous stalactites that project downward almost to the roofs of the buildings. The central structure that dominates everything is the hexagonal Palace of the Lord Thinkers (I learned the name much later, of course). It is higher and bigger than the seven buildings ringed around it, but what makes it stand out even more is the lettered sign erected on its roof. It's the largest illuminated sign I've ever seen. The displays on Times Square are nothing to it. It has no animation or figures, nothing but the angular letters of their curveless alphabet, formed of bars of glowing metal as thick as girders. I would guess each letter is two or three hundred feet high. The sign runs completely around the perimeter of the roof. Vovone translated it for me recently. It's their government motto: ALL THE HYDROGEN BELONGS TO ALL THE PEOPLE. This display illuminates the whole cavern with a nightmarishly bright orange that fades off gradually to blackness at the outer edges, where rings of illuminating metal on poles eke out the light. You can hardly look at the sign itself, it's so bright.

The people were thronging in front of another edifice (the Minor Task building, I later learned), where a great fluorescent...

[*Editor's note: Break in narrative.*]

...me the language, and find out everything he could about me. Those were the orders given to the Kaham Vove. He's a careful, methodical old gentleman, and he carried out the orders strictly and completely until he was arrested. While he was away on war duty Vovone substituted very well.

If I could overlook her greenish skin, and her dry-as-dust manner, and the whole sad situation I'm in, I suppose I could find Vovone attractive. She's small by the standards of her kind, but still an inch or so taller than I. I've always liked tall girls, so that doesn't matter. She has large, humorous brown eyes, long brown hair and good features. Her figure is somewhat lean and athletic, according to our ideas; but again, it happens I like that style. Or maybe I'm just getting lonesome. But there's no point to all this. She shows about the same interest in me as she would in a wild animal she was teaching tricks—wariness, briskness and a certain rough good feeling when I do something well. That's all.

They put me in two rooms that face the "street." One is a sort of workroom, which . . .

[*Editor's note: Break in narrative.*]

2

[Time in "Lomokome"—three pages]

. . . sunlight. They crave it. The great lens-and mirror-relay systems are engineering feats as complex and impressive as any of our aqueducts back home. They pipe sunlight into homes and buildings as we pipe water. The strong indoor glare bothered my eyes the first week or so and I wore my Raybans constantly, to their amusement. Now I'm used to it.

I believe the light that reaches them, even after the extensive relaying, is stronger than our natural sunlight, because there's no atmosphere at the surface of the moon to diffuse it and the whole relay system is under a high vacuum. They tell me that in their master lenses at the surface (which are as much as half a mile across) they use a crystalline organic compound that passes all the rays of the sun. I believe this, because I am becoming very tan. It's probably the last thing I expected when they were hauling me down into the black tunnel at the crater edge three months ago.

It's three months to a day, I believe.

I am almost certain today is 26 August 1954. I lost track of earth time in the first few weeks down here. Vovone explained their time system to me after a while, and by correlating in both calendars the date I was captured, I was able to figure out what day this must be.

They have no hours, but elaborate subdivisions of the day on the decimal system. Their day is the same as ours, a single rotation of the earth. It seems unnatural at first that they should fix on such a unit. But the earth's swift rotation is the most striking sight in their heavens, much more so than the transit of the sun, which is a tedious fifteen-day process. They use a lunar month of twenty-nine days, with an involved system of intercalated holidays to take up the slack of the fractions. Their long unit, called a *hasan,* is a period of nineteen years. One year is not significant to them. I remember as a plebe at Annapolis I had a Jewish roommate who told me that the Jews' lunar religious calendar squared away with the solar calendar every nineteen years. Maybe that proportion explains the odd length of the *hasan.*

They have ten months which they repeat cyclically throughout the *hasan,* giving the months new numbers with each repetition. Thus today is the 7th of Vislek-19, in the Hasan 1634. This number of the *hasan,* when you multiply it by 19, turns out amazingly high, and indicates that Lomokome history dates back at least 31,046 of our years.

One of the first questions I asked Vovone was what event the calendar dated from. She answered, "From the *Ayziet.*" The word is almost the same as

"Exodus" in our language. Then she told me, in rough outlines, their ancient history, which fades back like Japanese history into fantastic legends. There's this difference: she assured me that they have documentary evidence of all the events, including the *Ayziet* itself.

(I had no intention of wandering off into these details, but one thing seems to lead to another as soon as I get on the subject of the Lomokomians. I'll try to crowd their history into one paragraph and get back to the main track.)

According to Vovone, the Lomokome race is actually an ancient colony from the . . .

[*Editor's note: Of all the breakoffs in the "Lomokome" papers, this one is the most exasperating.*

Granting that the narrative is a systematic delusion, as all authorities agree, one still finds oneself strongly curious as to the origins of the phantom "Lomokomians."

It is the editor's opinion that the complete last phrase would have been "from the earth." The Navy authorities do not agree. But I can think of no other way in which Lieutenant Butler could have accounted for the obvious human appearance and traits of the "Lomokomians," which, though nowhere asserted, is assumed and implied throughout. I believe the "Ayziet" would have turned out to be the exodus from earth of the pilgrims from a lost antescriptural civilization that had mastered space travel.

Captain William Podell, USN, chief of Navy

psychiatry, is of the opinion that Butler's imagination failed him here—therefore he broke off and simply resumed his daydreaming at an easier point. Captain Podell states that this is quite usual in psychopathic fantasy-invention.

This accords with the over-all theory of the Navy: that there are actually few or no missing papers, and that Butler scribbled off what we have in bursts of semilucidity between intervals of torpor or delirium, picking up his fantasy at any random point. I am inclined to believe, on the contrary, that there may be hundreds of missing sheets, which Lieutenant Butler carried with him to his death. It is unlikely that this issue will ever be resolved.

We now come to the bulk of the continuous material, which I have divided into several sections for convenience of reference. There are no other sheets dealing with his first impressions. We are plunged into the middle of his main narrative.]

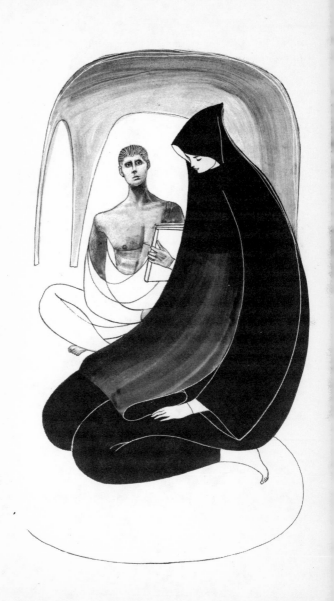

[War in "Lomokome"]

... pleasant enough, except that the place is somewhat dismal without the Kaham and Vovone. The "servants" were changed, as they are every month. The three of them are all male this time, and husky. There's no suggestion that they're guarding me—but that's what they're doing. I don't mind. I've no place to go and nothing to do until Vovone and her father return. Even if I escape I couldn't find my way back to the projectile without a guide, and anyway I can't take the plunge to the surface without an oxygen suit, which I don't have. It will be too bad if Projectile Two shows up while I'm ground-hogged down here. But my best estimate is that they can't launch it before 1 November, by which time I hope to have talked my way back to the surface, with the Kaham's help.

I hardly know how to go about describing the reasons for the arrest of Vovone's father. It is impossible, really, without quoting long sections of the Book of Ctuzelawis. When the war first began, Vovone herself gave up trying to explain it, and simply handed me the book. It was only after I read it and reread it, and visited the recruiting centers and the Task Board buildings, and saw the Death Cavern, that I began to understand what was happening, and to half believe it. Some of it still seems like a dream to me.

The whole concept of Death Day is so horrible and wild that I'm still not sure whether that part of it is allegory or fact. The reason for Kaham Vove's arrest is simply to determine whether or not he is eligible for Death Day.

I will try to describe the whole thing just as it has hit me. In its proper place I'll copy down Ctuzelawis, if my arm hasn't become useless from writer's cramp.

Long before I had completed the hypnotic language treatment, just as soon as a little sense began to emerge from the gibble-gabble of their speech (this was back in June, I think), I became aware that a war of some kind had either begun among the moon people, or was in the making. The war occupied a large part of the conversation between Vovone and Kaham Vove.

What baffled me was that Vovone seemed terribly worried that her father would have to go and fight. The Kaham is bent, weak and old, obviously of no military use. Beyond that, he is one of the nation's great men. The title "Kaham" is bestowed on the thirty-eight living Lomokomians pre-eminent in science. There can't be a thirty-ninth; a Kaham has to die before a new one can be named. I am in the custody of Kaham Vove so that he can make a report on me to the nation after studying and questioning me. From all this, it seemed to me no more likely that Kaham Vove would have to fight than that Einstein or

Bernard Shaw back home would have been drafted into the infantry. But the Kaham didn't laugh at Vovone. His end of the conversation, as nearly as I could make it out, consisted of assurances that he wanted to go, and had no fear of being killed, and so on—the sort of thing draft-age kids usually say when they're reassuring their families.

What made all this war talk especially hard for me to follow was their constant use of terms that were pure nonsense to me. They spent hours discussing in very worried tones things such as Major Tasks and Minor Tasks and Abstract Operations. I caught those phrases over and over, and others almost as often: Calculated Weapons, Morale Score, Formula Pilots, and still others, all meaningless.

I gathered that the enemy was a country called Lomadine. Up till this time I had had no instruction in their modern history, so I had no idea of the basis of the enmity. I did my best to eavesdrop during the following weeks. But though the language difficulty was clearing rapidly for me I was making no headway whatever in understanding the war talk.

One day a messenger arrived at the Kaham's house, dressed in the orange-and-white cloak of a government employee. He came into the room where the Kaham, Vovone and I were having our first meal after sleep (which is the big meal of the Lomokome day, oddly enough). The messenger handed the Kaham a note. The Kaham read it, looked very grave, and passed it to Vovone. She left the room and returned in a few moments with a small bag containing clothes for the Kaham, which she handed to the messenger.

The Kaham informed me that he was going to report for war service. He apologized for not having been able to complete my instruction systematically, but told me that I was now fairly well equipped for any activity in Lomokome. He commended me for working conscientiously at my tasks. Only one important element of my education remained incomplete, he said, and that was political orientation. He had hoped to handle that difficult matter himself, but now I would have to get it from books myself, under the supervision of Vovone. He left with the messenger, after telling Vovone that I was to read immediately a textbook of modern history for school children, and then the Book of Ctuzelawis. His last words to me I remember well. His wrinkled face took on a strange glow, and he said, "You will not completely understand Ctuzelawis at first. Persevere. He was the savior of our world, and probably the wisest and most humane being that the universe has ever beheld."

Vovone wasted no time. She took me to the reading room as soon as he was gone and snapped a microscroll into the machine. (These reading machines, which beat books all hollow for my money, are devices the size of a small camera, which can project print on a wall, or read a book aloud, or both. The books are transparent strips rolled into scrolls, on which are recorded both the sound and the printing. Four years of Annapolis studies could be compressed into a couple of dozen of these scrolls, altogether weighing less than one of our chemistry textbooks.)

Thereafter, Vovone was in charge of my education, and she did a thorough job of it, with a sort of frosty good nature. We were together most of the time, just the two of us alone in the house (except for the servants). But the question of a chaperon never seemed to arise. There was no need for one. I'd have felt like a grammar-school boy making a pass at his history teacher, even though her age, as I've calculated it out, is about the same as mine.

BY THE TIME the Kaham returned, two weeks ago, I was well informed about the war. It gave me a lot of pleasure to ask him questions and to debate about the amazing Book of Ctuzelawis. When he was arrested soon after, it was a real blow to me. We were friendly. He's made me understand a lot of things about his people. And I had high hopes that he would eventually get me permission to return to the projectile, and also some help to repair it. I haven't abandoned those hopes yet. He may still be freed.

To explain why he was arrested, I have to tell about the wars between Lomokome and Lomadine. I've been putting this job off. The whole thing is so strange that I don't know where to plunge in.

The story of Lomokome and Lomadine, which I derived from the school-age texts, was obviously slanted in favor of Lomokome. I can't guarantee the accuracy of the summary I'm going to put down. Since that time I've read a few scrolls designed for more mature readers (one or two without the knowledge of Vovone), but I've never found anything like an impartial description of Lomadine.

These two nations have divided the moon between them since Hasan 1531, which is just about the time of Christ in our reckoning. Moon history before that is a mess of the most horrible wars imaginable. In Hasan 1530, Lomokome and Lomadine allied themselves in a successful campaign to destroy Lozain, a civilized, scientifically advanced nation, the most powerful country on the moon, whose people, strangely enough, were cannibals—actual cannibals. There is no doubt of this. I asked Vovone a lot of questions about it. They habitually ate people.

Almost all the major wars in previous *hasans* had been started by Lozain for purposes of cannibalism, now against one country, now against another. The cannibals had shown the utmost political skill in playing off rival nations against each other. It was their practice to make a temporary alliance with one country while they forayed into another to capture human livestock; then in the next *hasan* they would assail their former allies and sign pacts with their former enemies. This practice was successful, unbelievable as it may seem, for several hundred years, during which the cannibals gradually destroyed or, more exactly,

ate up most of the nations on the moon. At last they felt so powerful that they simultaneously attacked both Lomokome and Lomadine, the two remaining great powers, who themselves had a long-standing enmity. The cannibals had cleverly exploited this hostility for generations, but they miscalculated at last. After the bloodiest war in moon history (up till that time), the cannibals were beaten. The victors utterly exterminated the adult cannibals, leveled their cities and scattered their young among the victors' territories. Lozain ceased to exist.

But no peace followed. Lomokome and Lomadine, with the whole moon to divide between them, began accusing each other of being cannibals like the extinct Lozains, and quarreling over a thousand small boundary questions. That, at least, is my interpretation. The Lomokome school text asserts that Lomadine made a "series of impossible and aggressive demands and began infiltrating in disputed territories, using the same cannibalistic tactics as the Lozains."

The schoolbook grudgingly admits, however, that "it is not quite fair to describe the Lomadinians as cannibals in the same sense that the Lozains were. Although their beliefs and their form of government show striking similarities to the culture of the cannibals, they probably do not actually eat human flesh." I gather that this reasonable view is due almost entirely to the influence of Ctuzelawis, and that before

his time both sides actually believed, or claimed to believe, that their enemies were true Lozains in practice.

A number of wars ensued between the two
nations, called the Universal Wars. These grew more
frightful in each generation. Those *hasans* that corre-
sponded to our early Christian Era were a time of
great scientific advancement on the moon. Both sides
evolved the uranium bomb in the same war, in our
year 347 A.D. It was soon rendered obsolete by more
powerful nuclear explosives.

During the Fourth War, Lomokome came
out with a nitrogen cloud, fissionable by remote means.
That was what you might call the daddy of them all.
To give you an idea: one nitrogen cloud could just
about obliterate the State of Massachusetts. The effect
of such a weapon was increased by the fact that it
was released in the huge caverns that constitute the
moon's habitable area, rather than in free space where
it could easily dissipate. It's interesting that Lomokome used *thirty-seven* nitrogen clouds against Lomadine before the surrender. It seems unbelievable. But
in centuries of warfare with nuclear explosives, these
moon people developed techniques for defense and
survival. What I've learned here certainly promises no
good for our future on earth. Some commentators
back home think the hydrogen bomb means the end
of war. But it seems that as long as people feel like
fighting they evidently manage to fight.

The Book of Ctuzelawis emerged shortly

after the Fourth Universal War, as a result of the terrible discovery about silicon, mentioned in the book repeatedly. Ctuzelawis is the great philosopher and prophet of the moon people. He unquestionably saved them from annihilation with his Law of Reasonable War. To me he seems a sort of combined Moses and Aristotle. To make his book understandable I must first try to describe the difference between the systems of Lomokome and Lomadine, which is at the bottom of all these wars, and which seems likely to continue to cause wars as long as time lasts.

If I were to put it in earth-terms, I would call it an "ideological conflict between Hydrogenism and Suggestionism." But no such words are used here. The Lomokomians refer to their mode of thinking as Orange; the Lomadinians are known as Blues. In this country it's a fighting insult to suggest that a remark has a Blue taint or that someone is Blue at heart. The exact opposite seems to be true in Lomadine. Orange is their favorite cuss word.

I don't profess to understand all the angles of these two systems. Both are based on philosophical reasonings, or assertions, that seem pretty foggy to me. The Lomadine setup is especially hard to grasp because all my knowledge of it has been filtered through the extreme prejudice and hatred of the Lomokome scrolls. But here is as fair a picture as I can present of both sides.

4

[*"Hydrogenism"*]

Hydrogenism, the social system of Lomo-kome, is founded on the scientific dogma that all things are hydrogen, or compounds of hydrogen.*

*(Note by Professor Robinson—This is a well-known theory in modern science. It was first promulgated in 1816 in the Annals of Philosophy by William Prout, an English chemist, and is generally referred to as "Prout's hypothesis." In a restricted sense there is truth in the view, as the work of F. W. Aston and others has shown, but strictly speaking it is a scientific metaphor rather than a fact. The St. Louis Journal-Herald has made much of this passage, claiming that it would have been impossible for Lieutenant Butler to stumble on Prout's hypothesis in improvising a fantasy. But I see nothing in the least unlikely in this, nor do my colleagues on the Rhododendron Project. Lieutenant Butler was a good chemistry student in the Naval Academy, and it is quite probable that he did enough random reading in the history of chemistry to come on Prout's hypothesis.)

They say no one thing is really any more or less valuable than any other thing, except in so far as it contains more or less hydrogen. There is a lot of

stuff about Mass Hydrogen and Energy Hydrogen which I don't follow, but it boils down to this: a thing is worth the number of hydrogen atoms transformed to produce it. Money, they say, is an unnecessary device that can be dishonestly handled to produce fake values; so they use no money. Private property is an absurdity, since no human force can add an atom of hydrogen to the universe or take one away. "All the hydrogen belongs to all the people" is the slogan on which their system rests.

Social justice, for them, consists in a fair distribution of hydrogen to everyone. By nature, they say, all men would try to use more hydrogen than they were entitled to. The function of government is to prevent such abuses. The ultimate question arises: "Who shall decide the apportionment of hydrogen?"

The Lomokomian answer is that the wisest men must decide. Thus has arisen the regime of the Lord Thinkers. The origin of this group is very obscure, but I gather that it was founded in a violent upheaval. The Lord Thinkers are a self-perpetuating body of thirteen supremely wise men, who theoretically are entrusted by the people with the fair allotment of hydrogen. They themselves appoint new Lord Thinkers as old ones die. They are responsible to no one, since by definition they represent the highest reasoning powers in the land.

Everything and every occupation in Lomokome has a hydrogen number, allotted by the Lord

Thinkers. The hydrogen number of an object, such as a chair or a house, is in effect its price. The hydrogen number of an occupation corresponds to the salary it commands. For instance: the hydrogen number of a master carpenter is 150. Every month every carpenter in Lomokome is credited with 150 (representing so many trillion or quadrillion atoms of free hydrogen, in theory). He can draw goods from the Lord Thinkers' stores and warehouses so long as he has a plus hydrogen balance. The hydrogen number of whatever he draws is charged against him. Every Lomokomian carries on his person a Hydrogen Book, in which his "salaries" and "purchases" are credited and debited by official government machines. The penalty for forging or tampering with a Hydrogen Book is death in a severe form: raking to pieces by red-hot steel combs. That seems to be the supreme crime in Lomokome—next to being suspected of Blue ideas.

In actual practice the Thinkers themselves do not allot numbers. This work is delegated to two bureaus—the Mass Hydrogen Bureau, which sets the number of objects, and the Energy Hydrogen Bureau, which fixes salaries. But the work of both bureaus is under the rule of the Lord Thinkers, who can modify numbers as they see fit.

The occupation having the highest hydrogen number is that of Lord Thinker—5,000. Next come the leading bureau heads, who get from 1,500 to 2,000. The scale descends gradually through government officials, industrial managers, scientists, artists, doctors and so forth, to the common people, the true "owners" of all the hydrogen. The highest number for any common workmen, allotted to uranium miners, is 175.

As the system works in practice, the hydrogen numbers allotted to objects no longer have much relation to hydrogen content. The numbers are simply fixed by the bureaus to maintain a balance between supply and demand. The numbers for occupations have become equally arbitrary. The Lomokomians themselves are surprisingly cynical about this aspect of the system. The cultivation of friendships in the Energy Hydrogen Bureau for the purpose of raising one's number is commonplace. They have an involved pun in their language as a byword: "Never mind the hydrogen of your job; it's the potassium that counts." Their word for potassium, *nipato,* is pronounced in the same way as the slang expression *Ni pata,* which means literally, "scratch my back," and figuratively, official connections or influence.

I've written nothing here but the barest outline of Hydrogenism. The way it works out in daily life is fascinating, but I can't stop to go into it. Yet the effect on marriage and family life is so odd that I can't help mentioning it briefly.

Since the people themselves are considered nothing but animated hydrogen, it follows that, like any other natural resource, they are owned by the community. Procreation is merely a job—with a rather low hydrogen number—since it requires little skill. It earns a bonus for married workers (women all work here, as well as men). A carpenter whose wife gives birth to a child is credited with an extra 50 for the month. The wife gets an extra 200, since it is considered that she did most of the useful work. The child is then taken away by the Lord Thinkers, like a chair manufactured by the parents, and reared communally. Rich people, however, who are sentimentally inclined, can rent their children back from the Thinkers at 25 a month, but it is impossible ever to acquire actual possession of them; for that, according to the Thinkers' doctrine, would be to reduce a free creature to slavery.

I use the term "wife" above, but actually there is no marriage in our sense. The sexual life under Hydrogenism is much too complicated to describe at this point in my story, but it is pretty fantastic. I can see now that if a visitor from the moon to the earth tried to describe our life he'd wind up writing an encyclopedia, and I have to avoid that temptation here. If I ever get permission to go back to the projectile, I'll take along a reading machine and a sackful of factual scrolls. And when I get back to earth the Navy can issue a 10,000-page report on Lomokome.

5

[*"Suggestionism"*]

I'm aware that I've done a none-too-satisfactory job of outlining the Hydrogen System of Lomokome, even though I've seen it in action and have all the scrolls I need on the subject. My description of the Lomadine way of life will probably be even poorer. I know nothing of it beyond what the Lomokomians have written about it. It's a little like trying to figure out what Christianity is all about, on the basis of a few hostile passages in Mohammedan books.

It seems that, theoretically, there is no government of any kind whatsoever in Lomadine.

The Lomadinians seem to be a religious nation. They maintain as their central belief that all governments and laws are immoral and blasphemous, because such institutions imply that God's creation is not adequate to run itself. Their entire system is organized around this principle, apparently to the last detail.

To find an excuse for some kind of community order, their philosophers have supplied a very strange line of reasoning. True, they say, it is irreligious for men to pass laws and to govern each other. But there is nothing wrong with the idea of people making *suggestions* to each other. In fact, it's a charitable way to act. Their country is run on the basis of Suggestions.

What amounts to a government is their General Welfare Suggestion Committee, whose 240 members are chosen by lot from among all the adults above a certain minimum level of age, education and intelligence. One quarter of this body is replaced every 500 days, so that there is a complete change in the board every 2,000 days. The Committee members select from among themselves, again by lot, a sort of president, who is known as the Suggester of Lomadine. His term of office is 1,000 days.

(The Lomokome writers exhaust themselves in sarcasm against this system. They call it "government by a lottery among idiots.")

Theoretically, as I say, there are, and there can be, no laws in Lomadine. But they do have a code of Standing Suggestions which, for all practical purposes, is a set of laws. They seem to have another code of Optional Suggestions, but I can't quite understand the purpose of it. The Standing Suggestions cover all the matters that criminal and civil law include back home. For instance, there is a Standing Suggestion that nobody kill anybody else for any reason, and another Standing Suggestion that everybody abide by a signed contract, and so forth.

A suggestion, in order to become a Standing one, has to be originated by the Suggester himself—

although anybody can suggest it to him—and approved by a majority of the Committee. It then passes into the volumes of Standing Suggestions, by which everybody is supposed to abide voluntarily. In theory there is nothing to prevent a man from disregarding any suggestion he pleases. Here is what happens when he does so. He is "invited to discuss" his behavior with a Discussion Panel. He states his reasons for disregarding the Standing Suggestion. If they seem inadequate, the Panel may vote to "suggest" that he be flogged.

Each Panel has two or three brawny members adept at flogging, which is by far the most common method of punishment in Lomadine. For certain offenses the Discussion Panel can refer the matter to the Suggester, who alone has the power to suggest that somebody cut off the offender's head.

I found it very hard to puzzle out this arrangement through the sarcasm and invective with which the Lomokome sources describe it. Maybe I've distorted it. The Lomokomians have a pat phrase—"the ridiculous mummery of Suggestions"—which they use in every reference to the system. As for the Optional Suggestions, these Lomokomian writers simply foam at the mouth and roll on the floor in hysteria, so to speak, at every mention of them. So I can give no adequate account of that aspect of Blue existence. Apparently, if a man violates an Optional Suggestion nothing at all happens to him. I gather that there are many more Optional Suggestions than Standing Suggestions. They seem to cover most of life. The favorite butt of the Lomokome writers is an Optional Suggestion about how to bathe. For all I know, that's a satiric invention; it's impossible to say. I know there are a great many Optional Suggestions about sexual life, which again furnish a lot of merriment to the commentators here. It seems that the Lomadine way is a rather prudish, old-fashioned monogamy, which is about the furthest thing possible from the practices of my Orange friends.

In Lomadine, private companies print money, handle the mails, build roads and do all the services usually performed by a government. They act in conformity with Standing Suggestions, which closely regulate their activities.

Even national defense is entrusted to a private company, in theory. But the head of this company is the Suggester, and the Suggestion Committee comprises its stockholders. There seems to be no purpose in this setup except to maintain the fiction that there is no government. It's obvious to me that this legal fiction dominates the whole life of Lomadine, and that it is maintained scrupulously from top to bottom of their social structure.

The Orange writers have a field day with all this lip service to a pretended freedom from government. They say that nothing can prevent a few individuals from hogging all the hydrogen in the country, and they declare that that's exactly what's happened.

They demolish very shrewdly the Blue fiction that there is no government. But all the same I can't help feeling that this queer no-government over there must work. The people can "suggest" it out of existence any time they want to. But they haven't, in many centuries. And after all, though I understand their manpower is somewhat less than Lomokome's, they've stood up to them in war time after time, winning about as often as they've lost. . .

Sixteen hours have passed since I wrote the last words. For some reason, as I was writing, a terrific wave of homesickness came over me. I went and did something extremely foolish. I took five of those tricky *kath* pills and knocked myself colder than a mackerel. I haven't taken more than two at a time before, and they gave me only a fine glow. I thought five were called for, the way I was feeling. It was a mistake.

I woke up dying of hunger and thirst. I'm writing now while I eat and drink, so as not to lose any more time. The cook, a six-foot-six fellow with a bushy beard, tells me that Vovone and the Kaham are coming home tomorrow, so I may not have much more time to write. Death Day has been proclaimed for the day after that. The cook doesn't know whether or not the Kaham has been ruled eligible. I said I guessed not, because otherwise he wouldn't be coming home. But the cook said no, that as a matter of fact everyone scheduled to die always spends the last night at home and walks to the Death Cavern with his family. It's part of the ritual. So I won't know, until they come back, how matters stand. It will be bad for me if . . .

[Editor's note: Break in narrative.]

[The Book of Ctuzelawis]

... simply copy down all of Ctuzelawis, if I can, translating as I go along. The language is extremely simple, so it shouldn't be too tough to do. Hope I have enough time to get it all down.

The Book of Ctuzelawis

In the days before the Fourth Universal War there was a man of Lomokome named Ostove, eminent in wisdom of metals. He explored the surface of the moon, alone at will, by order of the Lord Thinkers.

He was seeking rare metals in the Gray Sea when he encountered a lone woman of Lomadine named Norlen. She was an astronomer, and spent much time on the surface.

These two fell in love. They determined to marry.

The great enmity burned high in those days, and death would have befallen them had they returned to either land. They resolved to live their lives in hiding, on the surface. Because they were wise and resourceful they did so, and throve. They lived long *hasans* and had a son whom they named Ctuzelawis—that is, "Would-that-wars-would-cease." Then they died, and Ctuzelawis was left.

His parents had taught him all their wisdom. He lived a very long time alone on the surface. By stealth he visited the inhabited caverns, and found them full of folly and useless striving. He chose to remain in solitude.

In the fifth *hasan** of his life the silicon reaction was discovered in Lomokome and Lomadine.

**(Note by D.M.B.: Five* hasans *equal 95 years. Ctuzelawis was therefore somewhere between seventy-six and ninety-five years old when he wrote the Book.)*

When Ctuzelawis learned of the silicon reaction, his heart was troubled for the people in both lands, for he saw that destruction would soon swallow them, leaving not one alive.

Ctuzelawis therefore summoned strength to write a book that would show the people the way to escape the doom.

With much labor he wrote the book and finished it and copied it and sent copies by stealth through both lands.

When the people in both lands heard the words of the book they rejoiced everywhere.

At last the rulers heard of the book and demanded to see it. The Book of Ctuzelawis pleased the rulers very well also, for neither did they want to die, yet they saw death at hand.

Therefore in a Great Council—there had not been such a council in the time before, nor will there be such a council again in time to come—the Lord Thinkers of Lomokome and the Suggestion Committee of Lomadine met on the surface, with pomp and feasting and friendly words.

They agreed swiftly that they would live forever under the Book of Ctuzelawis.

They appointed officers and appropriated money or goods, each side after its own laws and manners, to fulfill every word of the Book.

So it was done, and so has the Book prevailed until this day.

Now these are the words of Ctuzelawis, which he sent to the two nations in the Hasan 1583, in the month of Ba-5, which was seven months after the discovery of the silicon reaction. This is the Law of Reasonable War. This is the Book of Ctuzelawis—which is the First Law of Lomokome by order of the Lord Thinkers, and the Unalterable Standing Suggestion of Lomadine by Murant, the Three Hundred and Fourteenth Suggester of Lomadine—prevailing in both nations from the first day of the first month of the Hasan 1584.

1.

I am Ctuzelawis, born of a father of Lomokome and a mother of Lomadine, Ostove and Norlen. I have lived my life alone on the surface, as my mother and father did.

Now I have spent my days and am very old.

It matters little to me that my dry frame should persist during a few more spins of our huge wondrous moon. I have filled my eyes with seeing and with study. What wisdom our world has, I have. It is time that I go down to my everlasting house.

But in fear of God I cannot but write these words. It is a great evil that men should destroy a world. It will not go unpunished. Nor will he go unpunished into whose heart God puts good words of advice, but who is too lazy or too timid to bring them forth.

My brothers, the end of days is at hand. The doom of the silicon reaction is sure. It is not a weapon. It is a wildfire of matter. It is a swift leprosy of the stuff of our world.

Lomokome and Lomadine now have the knowledge and the engines to start the silicon reaction. In time they will war again. Who doubts that this destruction is written for us?

We are all dead. Our wise men have found the skill to dissolve the globe in which we live. When have we failed to rush to use every skill of destruction in our wars?

Only read my words and lay them to your hearts, my brothers of Lomokome and Lomadine, and it may be that the world will yet be saved.

But if you will not heed me, but will say, "What is all this talk of Reasonable War? Who ever heard of such a thing? As for Ctuzelawis, he is a man

of no country, and a fool. Why should we listen to
him?" then you will proceed to the suicide of the race
in your greater wisdom. But I will have set these words
before you, and you will at least have had a choice
between death and life.

2.

You will say, "We have heard these alarms
before. The world's end has been promised for a
hundred *hasans*. But our fathers lived, ate, drank,
loved and died, and so do we. And so will our children, despite the silicon reaction."

Ask your men of wisdom what the silicon
reaction means. But you will not believe them when
they tell you. Wisdom is good, wisdom is to be praised,
when it gives you food, warmth, luxury and skill in
shedding enemy blood. Wisdom is a nagging wife
when it crosses you in your convenience.

But come and consider. The pleasant world
that you enjoy so much, what is it but matter? What is
it but a chaos of atoms, held together in solid forms
and orderly courses by the laws of nature? God has
given us the wisdom to pierce the secret of these laws
one after another. Was it not sure to come in time that
we master the law that binds our world into a solid
globe?

Our end is upon us.

How can it be stayed?

3.

Beware, my brothers, beware of the lying hopes that have led our race from war to war.

You will say, "Let us make a treaty. Let us swear to each other that neither of us will ever grasp the weapon of silicon in wars to come."

And you will write the treaty and sign it with both hands. And you will rest peacefully in the shelter of the words, as though they were stronger and thicker than very thick steel walls. And destruction will drop on you as it did on your fathers and on their fathers. And in rage and panic you will loose the silicon on your enemy if he has not already destroyed you and himself with it.

4.

Or you will say, "War now becomes foolishness. Let both sides destroy all their weapons of war. Let them make no more. Let them forbid the study of war in all their boundaries."

And you will argue and procrastinate. You will destroy some weapons and conceal others. But neither side will destroy the engines of the silicon reaction. And the stab of destruction will come while you sleep.

5.

And if not these, you will be beguiled by the folly greater than all these.

You will say, "Let us have a world government to keep peace. Are not all men brothers? Instead of two great nations at each other's throats, let us become one nation. Then there can be no wars, and the danger will be averted."

But a world government to keep peace is impossible because nobody wants it. That is the plain truth to which we have all been blind. War is no evil. We love to say it is, but we do not believe it.

War is necessary to us.

6.

Now you will say, "Ctuzelawis is a madman. Who does not know that we hate war? War is the curse of our world. Would that we could abolish it."

So you say. So you have always said. But in your words there is no value, for you do not know yourselves.

You need war as you need food.

Until you understand this, there is no hope.

If you say, "No, no, but war can be abolished by a world government," I swear to you that the silicon doom will destroy you before one *hasan* has ended.

War cannot be abolished.

War *can* be controlled.

I give you a law to control war.

If you will take this law to your hearts, if you will make the Law of Reasonable War your law, you will avert destruction.

This will be the sign that God has turned merciful to you in the last hour: that you will accept the Law of Reasonable War.

7.

What is a war?

It is a difference among nations, settled by a contest of destruction.

In order for war to exist, there must be nations, or a nation divided within itself.

There must be a difference that cannot be settled with words.

And there must be destructive power in both enemies.

Our race has been trying to end wars by eliminating one or the other of these things.

We have tried to unite all nations into one, so that there would be no enemies.

We have tried to create tribunals that could settle with words all possible differences among nations.

We have tried to agree to jettison all means of destruction.

We have tried all these things singly and together. We have tried them in many forms. We have shaped and reshaped the unions, the tribunals and the agreements.

Always we have failed.

Which of us believes in his heart that another shuffling of the preambles, the charters and the treaties —another juggling of words and promises—will save us from the doom of silicon?

It is time for us to acknowledge the truth that cries to us from the pages of our weary long history. Our race needs war. Our one hope lies in controlling war so that it will not destroy our globe.

The Law of Reasonable War is the only answer.

8.

We must have enemies. We cannot be happy without them.

This is a strange new idea, but consider if it is not so. Our enemies are the salt of our days. As the animals must sharpen their teeth on bone, wood or stone, so we must sharpen our powers, our ideas and our resources on someone we hate. It is true in the lives of each of us, and it is true in the lives of the nations.

If we have no enemies, we must invent them.

Consider the enmity by which our world is riven.

We say that it is impossible for the Hydrogen system and the Suggestion system to exist side by side in peace. On both sides we exhaust ourselves calling each other slaves and cannibals.

In our hearts we know that this is mostly

lies, but we go on uttering the lies. Why would we do this, if it were not for the desire to have an enemy?

What is the real difference between the two systems? When the clouds of words are blown away, they are simply two ways of making and sharing the goods of a nation.

Both have advantages. Both have drawbacks. There is no cannibalism on either side. These are hot words used to whet our natural appetite for enmity.

Which system is more just and more truly free? Words could be piled on either side until time ends. I, Ctuzelawis, will pass no judgment. I cannot. The doom of silicon is too close. Evidently the Hydrogen system suits the people of Lomokome, and the Suggestion system suits the people of Lomadine.

No people endures for long a way of sharing its goods that does not satisfy it. Each nation has its tastes and ways, developed in many thousand circuits of the sun.

But we do not have the choice, my brothers, between two systems or one, even if one system is all unjust. Our choice is between two systems, or silicon death for all.

It is said that the two systems are bent on destroying each other. That is true. But it is not because they cannot exist on the same globe.

If we were naturally inclined to peace, the two systems might work away side by side until the sun grew cold. But we are not inclined to peace.

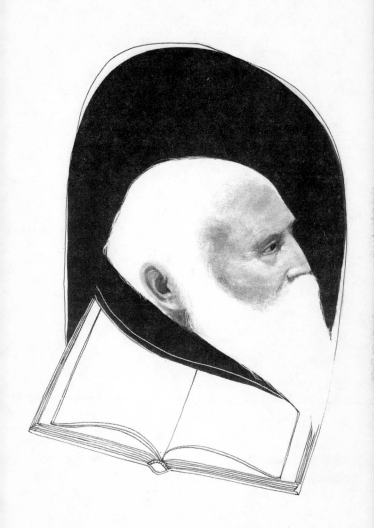

That is the truth about us. Let us first know the truth; then wisdom can help us.

Having an enemy is pleasant and healthy for our natures. It makes us alert and hard-working. It increases our attachment to our own land and dear ones. It drives us to explore and use all the resources of the land. It brings out the best of our qualities: self-sacrifice, ingenuity, love, charity and loyalty.

An enemy makes of us what religion is supposed to make of us, but never does.

Perhaps in a remote age, religion will penetrate our hearts to replace enmity. Would that it might be tomorrow! Then there would be no need for the Law of Reasonable War. But with the doom of silicon upon us, we cannot fool ourselves. Religion in our lives is words and books. Our true faith is still in enmity. Enmity between men, enmity between nations, is the power of all our days.

Therefore we need war.

9.

War has many uses and charms, which we must preserve in any law we make to control war.

There must be a final way of settling differences between nations. War does this. No substitute can satisfy. We all have soft, vulnerable bodies. There is no simpler and more final way to end a difference than to smash the bodies of those who differ with us. It would not suit us to smash all the bodies of the other side, for that would deprive us of our enemy. In war, therefore, we wisely smash only enough bodies among our opponents to convince them that they had better give up the dispute for the moment.

Consider, again, that our wisdom in protecting health and producing food is crowding our globe. Too many of us live too long when there is peace.

War effectively crops the race from time to time. Also, by destroying the young and the fit, it slows down the progress of science, and thereby the whole crowding process.

The Law of Reasonable War retains this useful feature.

A time of war is exceptionally zestful, joyous and productive. There is nothing like the intoxication of self-sacrifice, hard work and loyalty brought on by a declaration of war. There is no other way, considering what we are, not what we might wish to be, to bring about such mighty scientific advances, such piling up of goods, such searching of our minds, such hardening of our bodies, such general excitement, well-being and prosperity. True, these delights bring sorrow close upon them. But it is clear that the delight outweighs the sorrow. For we never hesitate to declare war again when the time comes.

The Law of Reasonable War preserves all these joys and eliminates much of the sorrow.

10.

Any war, controlled or not, reasonable or not, must have certain elements or it is not a satisfying and conclusive battle.

There must be a contest. Whole nations must strain to the breaking point to produce the means of destruction.

There must be large numbers of people killed.

One side must gain the right to impose its will on the other.

The Law of Reasonable War provides these elements. It provides them systematically and fairly. And it ends the risk of silicon doom.

11.

The part of war that we all sincerely regret, much more than the sorrow, is the waste of it.

If the end of war is to smash bodies, we must agree that in its present form it is not efficient. A huge expense for destruction on one side is always countered by vastly costly means of defense on the other. These almost cancel each other. Only the tiny margin of difference between them does useful work. A man can be killed at almost no cost, ordinarily. But in war the average cost of killing one man is more than the cost of building homes for ten thousand men.

The Law of Reasonable War completely eliminates this waste. This alone should recommend it to men's minds, aside from its much greater virtues.

12.

I, Ctuzelawis, alone under the black sky and the blazing stars all my life, have thought deeply about these things. I understand war. I understand our race. I would not mock you or jest in the shadow of death. It will need some words to expound this law—not many, for it is a simple idea. But you must patiently allow me to have my say.

I am proposing the only way to avert the end of the world. The only way, I say, except for a turning to God in the hearts of men. If I predicted such a change in our time you would be right to call me mad. Where is there a sign of it? But I am being sensible. I say there is no hope for such glittering news. I offer a law that will keep men alive as they are— loving war, desiring enemies and ignoring God.

13.

War is a contest. The side with the greater total effort wins.

The only measure we now have is an exchange of destructive force between the two sides.

But supposing an all-wise and all-seeing judge were available to measure the efforts on each side. He could predict the outcome. He could gauge the extent of the victory. It would not be necessary that a bomb be thrown or a shot fired, to find out who must win.

The measuring of effort against effort is the essence of war. The exchange of violence is necessary only because we have never had a better measuring instrument. Everybody knows that it has been a wasteful, crude yardstick.

Now, with the discovery of the silicon reaction, this measuring instrument becomes too dangerous to use. But worse than that, it now becomes meaningless. Both sides can produce infinite destruction at small cost. The next exchange of violence will end the world, without performing its function of measuring effort and awarding victory.

Yet we must have war.

The dilemma seems insoluble, but it is not.

We need a new measuring instrument that will fairly judge between two war efforts, replacing the exchange of violence.

I give you this new measuring instrument —the Law of Reasonable War.

14.

There shall be created at once a great college of wise men, drawn in equal numbers from Lomadine and Lomokome. They shall have the highest knowledge of all the sciences and arts of war. They shall come from every branch of life that feeds war efforts. There shall be men great in knowledge of physics, metals, agriculture, military strategy, chemistry and all other means of battle between nations.

These men shall cease to be citizens of their countries. They shall retire to the surface of the planet and shall live out their lives there, as I, Ctuzelawis, have done. They shall be fed and housed and supported by equal appropriations from both nations.

This college shall be perpetuated by adding to it in every *hasan* a small number of the most brilliant children from each country. These children shall go to the surface in their 100th *dahla* (aged eight years—D.M.B.) and shall be raised by the college. There they shall grow up, marry, have children and die.

If their children are of the highest promise they shall remain in the college. Otherwise they shall return to the caverns—either to Lomokome or Lomadine, as they shall elect.

This college shall be known as the College of Judges. Its purpose will be to make possible the waging of Reasonable War.

15.

There shall never again be a shot fired or a bomb exploded in war anywhere on our globe. Otherwise, wars will continue exactly as before.

Wars shall be declared.

Wars shall be fought.

Weapons and explosives and the supplies of wars shall be feverishly produced.

Many people shall be killed.

The side with the stronger war effort shall triumph.

The loser shall endure the bitterness of defeat.

The measure of the war efforts, however, shall not be the exchange of destructive force. For all men know now that the measure is wasteful and outmoded and must lead straight to the end of the world.

The measure will be the verdict of the College of Judges.

The College will inspect, test and compare the war efforts, and award the victory.

16.

Who can enforce this verdict?

Will the College have armed power?

The College will have no armed power.

But each side is already armed with the silicon reaction.

What can the defeated nation do, when the verdict is passed? It can accept, or it can attempt actual war. It knows already, from the verdict, that it cannot win an exchange of violence without silicon. And silicon means suicide of the race.

Will the loser not bow, and hope to fight another day, as nations have done since blood was first spilled among men?

You will say, what of the sudden attack? Despite the College, will not both sides pile weapons in secret as before? Will not one side make a great surprise onslaught, hoping to win quickly and own the world?

There is no surprise sudden enough to avert the answer of silicon. The dying lash of a surprised nation will be enough to break up the world in flaming dust. Both sides know this.

And so the verdicts of the College will stand. I swear to you by the courses of the stars that this is so. There is no other path for the nations.

Furthermore, men will soon see that the Reasonable War is so great an improvement over the foolish costly war methods of former days that they will desire no more. The first Reasonable War will establish the Law forever in the esteem and affection of the world.

17.

Under the Law of Reasonable War, differences will continue to arise between nations that cannot be ended with words.

Both nations will act as they have always done. Quietly they will begin to pile up materials and to train their men. As soon as one side thinks it can defeat the other, it will declare war.

The College of Judges will immediately assume supervision of the war, and set about reaching a verdict.

18.

In what way will the College reach a just and unmistakable verdict? What will count in its judgment?

Time was when valor of young men settled the issue. Weapons were puny and indecisive. The stoutest hearts and muscles won the day.

But between great nations of our time, valor on one side is hardly of avail against more and better machines, fuel and food on the other. It is a contest of manufacture and supply.

The College will set tasks for both sides to fulfill in the fields of manufacture and supply. The success with which each side meets the tasks will weigh most in the verdict.

There will be no need for exhausting, helter-skelter heaping up of all things useful and useless, such as we have had in wartime.

There are in every war great and small tasks of production. The great tasks are the old tools of war: metal, weapons, explosives, lumber, vehicles, fuel, grain, meat and such things. The small tasks arise from scarce substances or devices, which suddenly are greatly needed: manganese, diamonds, vanadium, lenses and the like.

Both countries will bend their whole efforts

to excelling in these tasks, as before. But they will be able to do this more simply and efficiently because there will be a definite number of tasks, not a hopeless maze of them.

When war is declared, the College will at once promulgate three Major and ten Minor Tasks. Their nature will be secret until the moment of announcement. Both nations will plunge into the production race at once, to manufacture and supply these things.

From time to time during the war the College will add other Tasks, Major or Minor, without warning. The endurance and adaptability of each side's war machine will be fully tested. The College will fix the time limit, but neither nation will know when the last moment will be until it arrives. Then the word will go out. The war efforts will cease. The College will measure the achievements on both sides and begin to compute the victory.

This simple, fair system will replace the foolish, agonized, largely wasted efforts of olden times. In peace, both nations will keep production of the needful things of life at a high level, for there will be no way to know which necessity may become a Task in the next war. There will be no need to waste substance in caring for a huge, sterile armed force. Until the moment of war all men will enjoy the benefits of abundance.

After war they will also benefit. For there will be nothing to do with the piled-up achievements

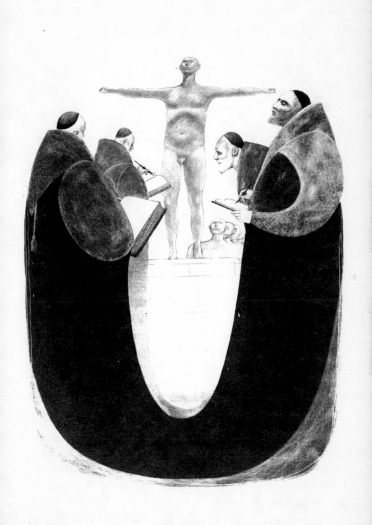

of the Tasks, when all is done, but to give them back to the people.

During war, suffering will be much less. The nations will not be bleeding themselves of every known substance to be expended in destruction. The College will set only enough Tasks to make a fair, hard war of it. What need for wearisome repetition of the same measuring device?

In old-fashioned war, to achieve a measurement, every resource must be thrown higgledy-piggledy into the general destruction.

But in Reasonable War the College will merely sample the productive strength of each side until the verdict becomes clear. All the rest of the waste of war will be avoided.

Will not the result of every war be the same?

No. For as always in history, the victors will incline to luxury and sloth, so their strength will decay. Losers will harden and improve themselves against the day of revenge. In old-fashioned war the same enemies have fought many times, and victory has passed from one to the other. So it will be in Reasonable War.

19.

But other things count in war besides such tasks. Those things will be measured too, and will affect the verdict.

In the old wars there was always a chance

of upsetting the whole balance of forces by discovering a new weapon. This element of ingenuity actually won wars despite inferior manufacture and supply.

The search for new weapons ended in the silicon reaction. In a continuation of the old wars, further quest would be absurd.

But in Reasonable War both sides will set their best minds working to calculate new destructive uses of the forces of nature. These new weapons need not be made. They will merely be calculated. The College will examine the calculations of both sides. It will award the proper weight, in reaching a verdict, to the side that has devised the most novel and usefully horrible exploitation of natural laws.

20.

Wise men do not seem quite sure whether military skill has any effect in the outcome of wars. It is argued that a sufficient advantage of food, metal, fuel and explosives on one side means victory. Military strategy, it is said, merely sets the dates and places where the victory shall become a matter of record.

But this may not be quite so. Perhaps a fool in command could fritter away a great advantage by fouling its use against the enemy. Nations in the past have often lacked the sense to make the best and the cleverest men their leaders.

The College will therefore examine battle

plans drawn up by tacticians and strategists of both sides. It will submit these leaders to tests of Hypothetical Battles, wherein they will be called upon to make many critical decisions.

In reaching a verdict the Judges will penalize lack of military judgment on either side, and will reward exceptional thoroughness or brilliance.

21.

While valor has become unimportant, Willingness to Die has not. In our present wars, it is still necessary to find young men to work the machines. A man may be a coward, but if he has the self-control to work a machine under fire he is as useful as a hero.

Noncombatants also have to be willing to die in towns and factories.

Therefore the Judges will also measure Willingness to Die.*

*(Note by D.M.B.: At first I translated Willingness to Die as "morale," but it didn't seem quite the same thing. So I left it in the literal form.)

22.

It is necessary that people die in war—even in a Reasonable War.

Slaughter is the great deterrent of warfare. Without it, war is so delightful, so gay, so exhilarating, so productive, that the nations might well battle forever. But sorrow in time saps the will to fight. And the burying of large numbers of young men makes war less practical for a few years, until a new crop grows. Also it slows the crowding of the globe.

Perpetual war we do not want. Like perpetual intoxication, it would lose its savor and become a trouble. The nations, with folk wisdom, rarely indulge in the pleasant strain of war more than once or twice in a generation.

The great danger of Reasonable War is its economy, practicality and fairness. It is a temptation to have wars all the time. This would blunt the instrument of Reasonable War and lead back to silicon.

I urge you therefore, my brothers, to be strict and unchanging in your observance of Death Day.

At the end of a war, the College of Judges shall calculate the number of people that shall die on each side. This number shall be proportioned to the general verdict. It shall be large enough to render victory painful and defeat disastrous.

The governments of each side shall thereupon slay the required number of their own people, young and old.

Do not shrink at the seeming cruelty of this portion of the Law. It is the cornerstone of Reasonable War.

And I say to you, is it really cruel?

A government that declares war now, whether in aggression or self-defense, by that act sentences to death a certain part of its people. The stroke of the pen that signs the war document is a knife stroke, butchering thousands. We all know these things.

Reasonable War brings clarity and order to what exists—to what must exist, until men change in spirit. It eliminates waste and chance. It reduces a foolishly chaotic arrangement, which threatens our total destruction, to a sane, safe, workable process.

23.

Who shall die? Those who are willing.

This is the manner in which the Judges shall measure Willingness to Die.

Immediately upon an outbreak of war, emissaries of the College in each country shall open death offices. Young men shall come to these offices and volunteer to die upon the verdict.

At the end of the war, the number to die on each side shall be fixed by the College. The dead shall be elected by lot from among the volunteers. There shall be no reprieve from Death Day.

This will be the test of the Willingness to Die in each nation. The numbers that volunteer, and the speed with which the rolls are filled, will decide the weight of this part of the war effort in the verdict of the Judges.

If a government tries, openly or in secret, to force young men to offer to die, the judges will award victory in the war to the other nation. For that will be a clear sign of a feeble national spirit.

The side with the bravest and best young men will fare better. This is proper in war.

But a certain number of older people die in war too. At present this is simply decided by the random dropping of missiles.

In Reasonable War, justice and common sense must replace the chaos of chance.

The College will proclaim the numbers of old people that are to die. The old will be named by the government from among those who have led the war effort: scientists, militarists, industrialists and the like. For it is only just that they who held the power to win or lose the war should bear the brunt of the outcome.

This system will encourage bravery in the young and the mightiest exertions in the old.

The young, by offering to die speedily and in great numbers, can turn the scale of victory and thus save many of themselves from death. The old will press the war effort as they have never done until now. Their heads will be at hazard.

All will die in a great immolation in the presence of their heads of government, with due pomp of sorrow, on the day following the verdict of the Judges. This will be known forever as Death Day.

24.

I, Ctuzelawis, am weary. My hand grows

cold. My frame has little moisture. I shall live, as I feel the will of God, to send these words I have written to the nations. But even as you read, I shall be taken.

Read this Law with diligence. There is much to be interpreted, much to be expanded. But in the words I have written you will find the rule and the spirit to control wars.

Establish the College of Judges, at once, and pledge your souls to accept their verdicts. They will be the custodians of my Book. They will interpret it to you. Out of its words they will give instructions and judgments.

25.

These are the blessings that will come to you by obeying the Law of Reasonable War.

You will be able to fight each other to the end of time. You will have the delights and stimulation of everlasting enmity. But the sorrows of war will be kept within decorous bounds.

You will prosper, for you will continually be busy. When war may come at any time, the nations will not neglect useful arts, nor the training and health of the people.

You will be rich, for you can turn all your industry to the making of good things in peacetime. You need only keep your factories and farms working, ready to assume war tasks. When war is declared the

College will set Major Tasks of weaponmaking, and then the nations can gut their stores of metal and exhaust their peoples in a race to heap up these useless things. When the race is done and the verdict passed, you will have the unused heaps intact, ready to melt down again into things that are needed. You will not burn and smash and explode the fruit of your terrible war toil, as in former days. You will enrich, not impoverish, yourselves by each war effort.

You will live in quiet and safety. The damage that war can do will be bounded, not boundless as in the old days. The great fear, the fear that has soured your lives for many *hasans,* the fear of new weapons, will be laid. You will waste no substance making new weapons. For the idea, the formula on paper, is what truly matters, and only that will count in the victory.

But the blessing above all blessings is that you will live on, and never be destroyed in a great calamity. Death in war you will have. But it will be a reasonable slaughter. Its extent and its victims will not be decreed, as in former days, by luck and disease. Instead the right people will die in the right numbers. There will be no risk of the spread of destruction beyond the desired extent.

This is Reasonable War, my brothers, the wonderful law that Heaven has told me to set before you. Do not think that these are truly the words of feeble Ctuzelawis. But understand that these are words spoken by a Spirit, and written down by my old hand.

The curse that will come upon you if you set aside the law is this: fire, and great crashings, and the air turned to poison, and the ground burning and melting under your feet, and the swift end of all flesh and all things.

Farewell, with the prayers of Ctuzelawis.

Now THE FOUNDING of the College, with the words of the agreement, and all the things that came after the writing of the Book of Ctuzelawis;

And the Statutes of Reasonable War;

And the histories of the war;

These are all written in the Annals of Reasonable War, kept by the College of Judges until this day.

7

[*"Death Day"*—
Escape and Recapture: Five Fragments]

Well, that's the Book of Ctuzelawis, and my fingers are so cramped from copying it, my hand is stiff as a dead man's.

I can see Admiral Garrett's face when he reads my report, his eyebrows shooting up to the ceiling. They'll say I made up all this "balderdash." But my friends will know better, anyway. I got straight C's in English at the Academy. I could no more make up the Book of Ctuzelawis than I could swallow an elephant.

No, the book exists, all right, and it is the Bible of these people. Both countries really live by it. That is the strangest thing of all. But maybe, after all, they really had no choice.

I gather they once had something that more nearly resembled our Bible. The name literally translated is *The Gray Stone*, which is meaningless. I could never find out if it was a law code, or a scripture or what. There are no copies of *The Gray Stone* in Lomokome. It's forbidden reading. The encyclopedias refer to it in passing as "primitive Blue mythology" and "the poisonous Blue superstitions of *The Gray Stone*," and so forth, in their usual fashion. I don't know whether it

exists in Lomadine either. So far as Lomokome is concerned, the Book of Ctuzelawis is their law, and Ctuzelawis is their prophet. And if they have any god, it's Reasonable War.

I can't write much more now; glad I got the book copied, anyway. The Kaham returned just as I was writing that last paragraph. He is going to be executed in Death Day tomorrow, after all.

It seems he had been placed in charge of the New Weapons calculators, replacing another Kaham who died of old age during the war. Lomadine outscored Lomokome about two to one on new weapons, and I understand that the war was lost in that way, because the verdict was pretty even in all other departments. The Kaham's defense was that the College didn't really understand his weapon. But a committee from the College gave him a hearing, and insisted they had no trouble at all understanding it. It was a long-range paralyzing ray—and good enough, except that it could be jammed too easily. Lomadine, they tell me, came up with a poisonous microbe that resists every known antitoxin. The verdict looks damned fair to me, on that basis. In fact, the Lomokomians ought to thank God that they fought a Reasonable War, not an old-fashioned one, or they might have all been wiped out.

Ctuzelawis really had something.

The Kaham is prepared to die, but he's not satisfied. He claims the committee from the College was made up of a lot of juniors who couldn't understand the antijamming features of his ray. He says there are a couple of old masters in the College who would see his point if he could get to them. But there's no provision for such an appeal in the system.

I suggested that he make a break for the surface, go up to the College and see the old boys. He's got nothing to lose, that's obvious. I said I'd help him, if he'd get me a breathing suit. But he just laughed sadly. He said it made little difference to him when he died, except that he disliked leaving Vovone. She seemed a lot more taken with my suggestion than the Kaham.

So now they're both praying and going through some kind of complicated ritual. I don't know what happens to me after tomorrow, but I guess I'll find . . .

[*Editor's note: There is a noticeable difference in the handwriting on the rest of the sheets. This factor simplified the arranging process.*

Though the writing in all the papers is rather rough and hurried, from this point on it is hardly legible, due to haste, or weakness, or both.]

. . . useless. I don't know why I bother. Except that the old Navy log-writing habit is too strong to break. And anyway, since I reached the moon it stands to reason others will. I ought to leave some word as to what has happened to me.

It's a thousand to one, at this point, that we're finished, all three of us. The Lord Thinkers take

a mighty dim view of anyone who ducks out on Death
Day, and of anyone who helps him do it.

We're back at the projectile now. The College
is about nine hundred miles from the crater Copernicus, the Kaham tells me. My idea is to get the projectile
going again. The battering of the outer skin isn't important. The main repair, which the Kaham thought
he could do in an hour with materials he has, is . . .

[*Editor's note: Lieutenant Butler wrote here
some top-secret details of the Navy's extragravitational
propulsion system. Eight lines of writing, of no im-
portance to the narrative, are deleted.*]

. . . The long and short of it is, it doesn't
work, because of the impurity of his (*deleted*) crystals.
Even though it means curtains for me—in all likelihood
—I can't help being slightly amused. The Kaham has
been pretty damn' patronizing about the elementary
state of science in our world. But it seems we can still
show these wizards here a thing or two about the
separation and refinement of rare earths.

I just couldn't stand the horror of Death Day.
It was really I who talked the old man into bolting.

They have a special Death Cavern where
this ceremony is held. It's a huge rounded grotto with
a rough natural dome. At the top is a tremendous lens
that pours relayed sunlight, and all around the side
of the dome are similar smaller lenses. There's plenty
of light in the place, of a peculiar greenish-yellow sort.
The floor of the cavern is covered with acres of stone

benches, for perhaps two hundred thousand people or more. At the far end, a long wide flight of stone steps leads up to a platform cut into the rock. On the platform are more benches, and an immense block of stone that resembles an altar.

When we got there the place was almost full of people already, although . . .

[*Editor's note: Break in the narrative.*]

. . . not much blood from each individual. The drug they take just before mounting the platform seems to inhibit bleeding. Even so, with thirteen Lord Thinkers cutting about five throats a minute apiece, you have a lot of blood running off that altar into the gutter around it. This is drained by a little channel that cuts directly across the middle of the cavern floor, in a gentle downward slope, so that the blood keeps running. The people dip handkerchiefs into it all along the way—a part of the ritual, no doubt.

The worst horror of the whole business is that nobody seems to think it's horrible. It's like some huge college commencement, except that instead of shaking hands and getting a diploma when they come up, the boys get their throats cut. They run it off so smoothly, and everyone is so peculiarly gay and tearful at once, and there's such a holiday air about the proceedings, that you almost forget you're seeing people die. I must have seen fifteen thousand slaughtered before my eyes before we escaped, and it hardly affected me as badly as an auto accident I once saw.

I guess you can believe one person has died, but you can't believe in massacres, even when you see they're going on.

We were seated on a bench on the extreme left side, near the back. The bodies under their orange cloaks were wheeled past us in a steady parade, not a dozen feet from where I sat, on the way to the crematorium. There was some kind of sweet flowery perfume on them. Girls and boys about thirteen years old were doing the wheeling. I began to get the creeps.

I looked at the Kaham. He was watching calmly, but unconsciously he was wringing his hands. What amazes me as much as anything is the way they permit the condemned people to sit with their relatives until the last. . . .

[*Editor's note: Another break.*]

. . . desperate. I'm sure the Kaham didn't care about dying. But his reputation as a scientist was something else. He was willing to break an almost sacred law for a chance to redeem it. I'm sure that if we ever reach the College and they acknowledge he was right, he'll cut his own throat with pleasure.

The unbelievable freedom with which they run the ceremony made it easy for us to leave. We went straight to the Kaham's laboratory, where we got breathing suits. He had no trouble finding [*a deleted account of materials needed to repair an extragravitational propulsion system—Ed.*] The laboratory and the tunnels were deserted. Vovone brought out the *Dalka,* a buoyant sedan-chair kind of thing that floats just off the ground and is propelled by a simple jet engine. (Only high officials are allotted these gadgets, which have a colossal Hydrogen number that keeps them out of the hands of common people.) The Kaham calculated that the fuel would take us up to the surface or within a mile or so of it. So we piled in all the gear and shoved off, avoiding the main tunnels, flitting along through pitch-black unused caverns and galleries. The Kaham found his way by using a sort of compass and occasionally turning on a dim light when entering a new tunnel. He seems to know a hell of a lot about the interior of the moon.

When the air got too thin near the surface, we put on the breathing suits. It was a wonderful feeling, emerging from the crater into true sunlight again. When I saw the big greenish crescent Earth shining in the black sky I all but cried. The *Dalka*'s fuel lasted us right up to the projectile, and—

The Kaham thinks he has the propulsion unit ready to go.

[*Editor's note: The above sheet is half blank. Lieutenant Butler did not resume writing on it after breaking off. The next sheet was found crumpled up outside the projectile, wedged among stones.*]

. . . small hope, but it was worth trying. It's all over now. They came while we were taking apart the *(deleted)* chamber again. We knew they'd track us

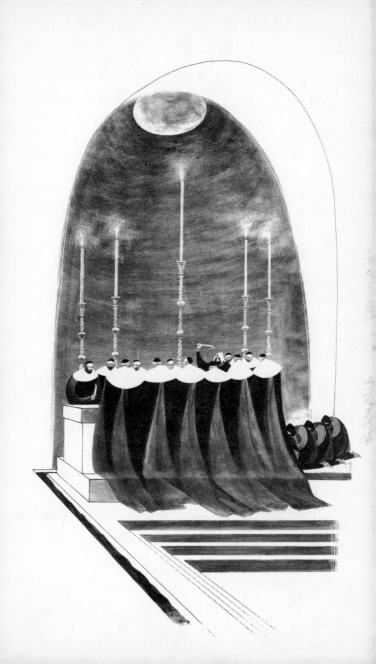

to the projectile ultimately, but it was our one chance.

Will they kill me? I don't know. The Kaham and Vovone are due for death of course—in an unpleasant form. But do you kill a giraffe for escaping from the zoo? That's what I am here, a sort of two-legged giraffe from a strange world. Maybe they'll keep me in chains hereafter. Or maybe they'll put me out of my misery because I'm too troublesome. I'll find out soon enough. I'm writing this while they dismantle the . . .

No more time.

[Editor's note: The next lines are printed in large shaky block letters.]

SMALL CRATER LEADING INTO TUNNEL TO LOMOKOME BEARS 225° RELATIVE TO PROJECTILE, DISTANCE ABOUT 12 TO 14 THOUSAND YARDS. BIG STONE A HUNDRED YARDS FROM ENTRANCE SHAPED LIKE A MUSHROOM LYING ON SIDE. ENTRANCE HARD TO SEE BUT...

[Editor's note: The above is the last of the "Lomokome" papers.]

Excerpt from Appendix D
of the Robinson Report
Flight Log of the Pilot of Projectile Two

Condition of Projectile One when found: outer shell bent, cracked and buckled, not seriously. Unsuccessful effort had been made to restore airtight integrity. Interior disorderly. Propulsion unit intact except for (deleted list of parts), which evidently were removed in repair effort. Did not find these in brief search. All instruments intact . . .

Reconnoitered extensively outside projectile for six hours. No sign or track of pilot. Followed directions found on sheet outside projectile. No sign of a crater at bearing and distance indicated, nor of mushroom-shaped stone. In view of possibility that projectile had shifted position and therefore relative bearing no longer accurate, flew seven slow circles near surface at distance indicated. Result of search negative.

At distance indicated, bearing 135° relative (almost in opposite direction), observed large sunken mass of rubble 500 yards wide, such as might be caused by cave-in of a fissure or crater. Made no attempt to dig, as very large-scale sustained effort would be necessary to obtain any results.

Numerous similar cave-ins, deep pits and fissures abound near projectile. Slanting sun did not illuminate deeply. Plumbed two pits with thousand-foot line without finding bottom. Others two and three hundred feet deep.

It is believed that Pilot Butler fell into one of these pits or fissures. Recovery considered extremely unlikely even with large searching party . . .

—HERMAN WOUK

About the Author

When I visited my Public Library the other day to see how the books of Herman Wouk were faring, I discovered that the available copies of *Don't Stop the Carnival* and *Youngblood Hawke* looked as if they had been hit by a hurricane. Now this library is one of the best equipped in Westchester County, New York, just outside Manhattan, and it takes care to keep its stock replenished. Its shelves carried novels of other authors in the "W" category, all of the books in pristine condition, so evidently there had been a bigger demand for Wouk's stories than the librarians had expected. His were not first editions by any means—those had been read to pieces long before, and had been replaced a number of times. Moreover, *The Caine Mutiny* was "out"—which speaks well for a novel fifteen years old that has been reprinted often and is available in paperback and the movies.

The shelf of Wouk books reflected industry, imagination, and diversity of themes and people, excellent qualities for successful storytelling. I observed that Wouk was not plowing only one field; he was making good use of what he had seen and heard, and every time he published a story he had a new setting, an unexpected plot, and a fresh attitude. His first novel, a lighthearted spoof of radio broadcasting called *Aurora Dawn,* reflected his experiences as a writer for the famous comedian, Fred Allen. The Book-of-the-Month Club selected it, something that seldom happens to first novels. He followed this with *The City Boy,* a warm comic novel evoking his own Bronx childhood; this book retains a special circle of admirers, both here and abroad. He achieved celebrity with his third book, *The Caine Mutiny*.

From naval procedures he turned to the ambitions and heartaches of a girl in mid-Manhattan and described an entirely different segment of metropolitan society. Done with *Marjorie Morningstar*, he moved to the calamitous career of a man with a powerful drive to live and write who is confronted by the competitive demands of book publishing: *Youngblood Hawke*. And then he turned to good use his leisurely reflections in the warm Caribbean air, where he had time to think about what a New Yorker gets out of a tropic paradise. It gave him an opportunity to view a characteristic predicament with good humor. This was *Don't Stop the Carnival*.

We meet another example of Herman Wouk's lively and disciplined imagination when we come to *The "Lomokome" Papers,* a document purporting to give the experiences of an American pilot on the moon. But the mere physical landing on the lunar surface, which has captivated storytellers for decades, is only the frame for a disclosure that challenges us to think earnestly about the direction human society is taking. Wouk uses three forms of narration to give substance to his fiction, first reproducing the formal verbiage of a confidential naval report; next transcribing the jottings of Lieutenant Daniel More Butler, USN, concerning the strange social organizations of Lomokome and Lomadine; finally providing in Professor Ctuzelawis' book a sharp satire on beings whom he finds "loving war, desiring enemies, ignoring God," and developing the Professor's theory of "Reasonable War," in which killing will not be haphazard, hit or miss, but regulated with computing precision—the final contribution of science to man's inordinate appetite for contriving his own misfortune.

It seems to me that the man who thought out this scheme is the Wouk who wrote *This Is My God,* a friendly, hopeful and reverent message that showed Wouk's reliance on the spiritual as a source of confidence and hope. Despair is not part of his nature, but indignation is, and *The "Lomokome" Papers* makes me believe that behind the cold, analytical blueprint of the Professor is the controlled anger of a man who wants his America to think seriously about the realities of human existence.

HARRY HANSEN